USBORNE BIG MACHINES
TRUCKS

Harriet Castor

D0843574

Designed by Robert Walster

Illustrated by Chris Lyon, Sean Wilkinson
and Teri Gower
Cover design by Tom Lalonde

Consultant: Gibb Grace
(Product and Environmental Affairs Manager, Leyland DAF Ltd)

Contents

 # Truck

Trucks are used for taking all sorts of things from one place to another. They often carry very heavy loads, so they need to have powerful engines and strong bodies.

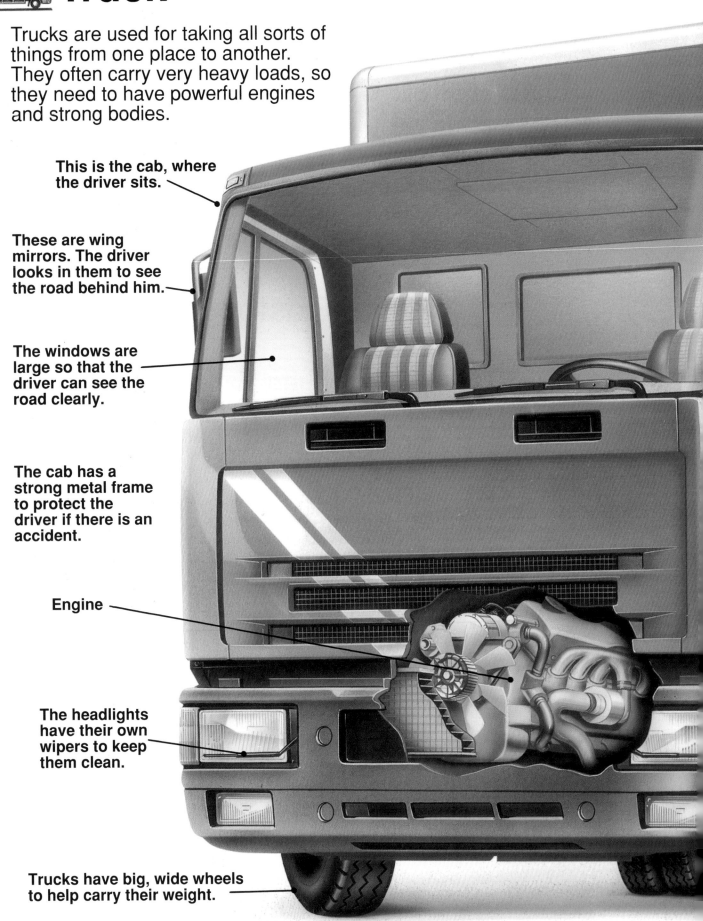

This is the cab, where the driver sits.

These are wing mirrors. The driver looks in them to see the road behind him.

The windows are large so that the driver can see the road clearly.

The cab has a strong metal frame to protect the driver if there is an accident.

Engine

The headlights have their own wipers to keep them clean.

Trucks have big, wide wheels to help carry their weight.

This is the body of the truck. The load is put in here.

The main frame of the truck is called the chassis. It is made of strong steel.

There are double wheels at the back for extra support.

Different bodies

This truck's body is like a big box. It has extra space above the cab.

This truck's flat body is called a flatbed. The load goes on top.

This truck has low sides which fold down to make unloading easier.

Engine check

Cab   Engine

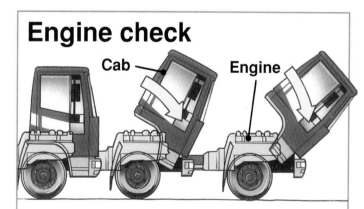

When the engine needs to be checked, the cab can be tilted forward. This makes the engine easy to reach.

 # Articulated and rigid trucks

There are two main types of truck: articulated trucks, or artics, and rigid trucks. Artics have two separate parts, which can be joined together and taken apart again. Rigid trucks are all in one piece.

On the body it often says who the truck belongs to and what is inside.

Artic

The two parts of the artic are linked. The link lets the cab turn first when it goes around corners.

The back part of the artic is called the semi-trailer.

The semi-trailer can stand by itself when these metal legs are put down.

The semi-trailer locks onto a big metal plate here.

The front part of the artic is called the tractor unit.

Swapping semi-trailers

Tractor unit drives away.

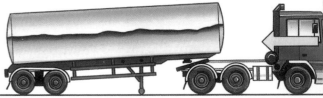

Tractor unit backs up to the new semi-trailer.

When the artic arrives, its tractor unit and semi-trailer are taken apart. The driver does not unload the semi-trailer. He leaves it behind.

A new semi-trailer is put on. Now the artic is ready for its next journey. This saves time, so the artic can make more deliveries.

Curtainsider

Here is one type of rigid truck. It has a special body, with sides that pull back like curtains. It is called a curtainsider.

This shaped panel helps the truck push through the air when it is going fast.

The sides of this truck fasten here with buckles.

The curtainsider is loaded by a forklift truck.

The curtains can be drawn back all the way along the sides.

Most trucks only open at the back. Curtainsiders are easier to load.

Tanker

A tanker has a body like a big can. Tankers can carry liquids, powders and gases. They often carry fuels such as petrol and diesel. This tanker is delivering to a petrol station.

The compartments stop the liquid from sloshing around too much.

This compartment has petrol in it.

Inside the tanker there are separate boxes called compartments.

This compartment has diesel in it.

These curved sides are stronger than the flat sides on normal trucks.

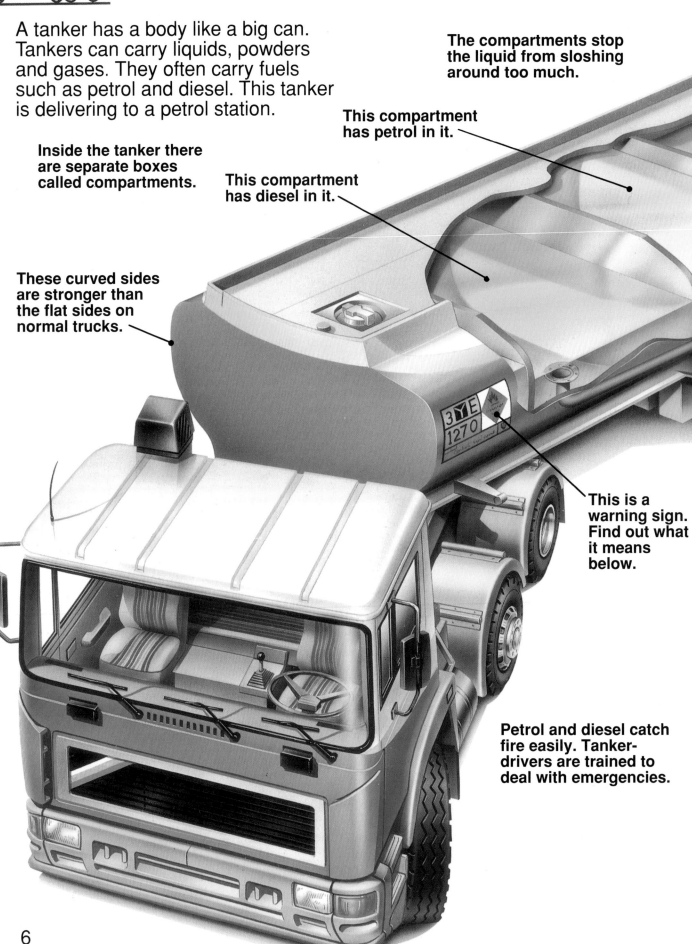

This is a warning sign. Find out what it means below.

Petrol and diesel catch fire easily. Tanker-drivers are trained to deal with emergencies.

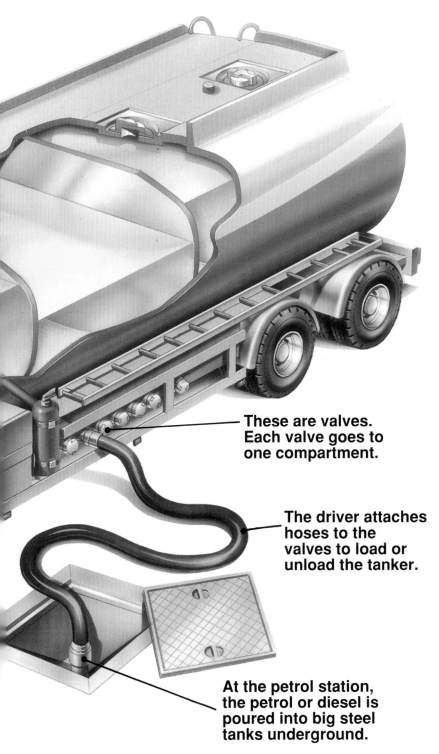

These are valves. Each valve goes to one compartment.

The driver attaches hoses to the valves to load or unload the tanker.

At the petrol station, the petrol or diesel is poured into big steel tanks underground.

Tanker delivery

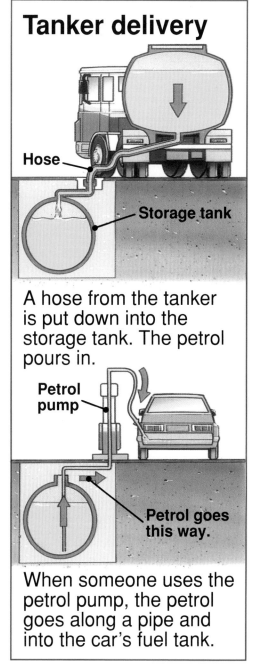

Hose

Storage tank

A hose from the tanker is put down into the storage tank. The petrol pours in.

Petrol pump

Petrol goes this way.

When someone uses the petrol pump, the petrol goes along a pipe and into the car's fuel tank.

Warning signs

Tankers have signs on them to show what is inside. Then if the tanker catches fire, the firefighters will know right away how to put out the flames.

FLAMMABLE LIQUID

A flammable liquid is one that can catch fire. This sign is used on fuel tankers.

FLAMMABLE SOLID

This sign shows that the load is something solid that can catch fire.

TOXIC GAS

This sign shows that the tanker is carrying a toxic, or poisonous, gas.

Dump truck

Dump trucks have bodies that tilt so that the load slides out. This giant dump truck is working at a quarry.

Dumping

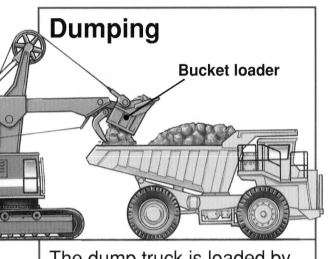

Bucket loader

The dump truck is loaded by a big bucket loader. It fills the back with rocks.

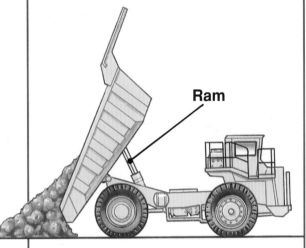

Ram

To empty the dump truck an arm called a ram lifts up the body. The load slides out.

Different dump trucks

Not all dump trucks are the same. Dump trucks of different sizes are used for carrying different loads, such as gravel, sand or fruit. Sometimes smaller dump trucks are called tippers. You can see three of them here.

8

This board protects the cab from falling rocks.

The driver climbs this ladder to reach the cab.

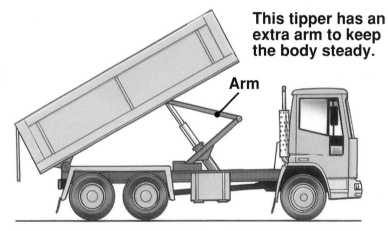

This tipper has an extra arm to keep the body steady.

Arm

This dump truck is too big to travel on normal roads.

The rocks are loaded in here.

This is the tallest truck in this book. Its wheels are twice as high as a tall person.

This slope stops the load from falling out when the truck is not dumping.

This tipper can dump its load sideways.

This tipper's extra long ram lifts the body up very high.

9

Wrecker

This truck is used when a car breaks down or has an accident. The truck can lift the car back onto the road. Then it can tow the car away.

This arm is called a boom.

The driver works the winch with these switches.

This cable is made of metal wire. It is very strong.

These metal rods are lifting rams. They hold the boom up.

These lights are used if the truck is working at night.

These metal legs dig into the ground to help keep the truck still.

Muscle power

The first wreckers just carried equipment. This one was used in 1914. The crew did the lifting themselves, with ropes, chains and a metal tripod.

Tripod   **Wrecker**

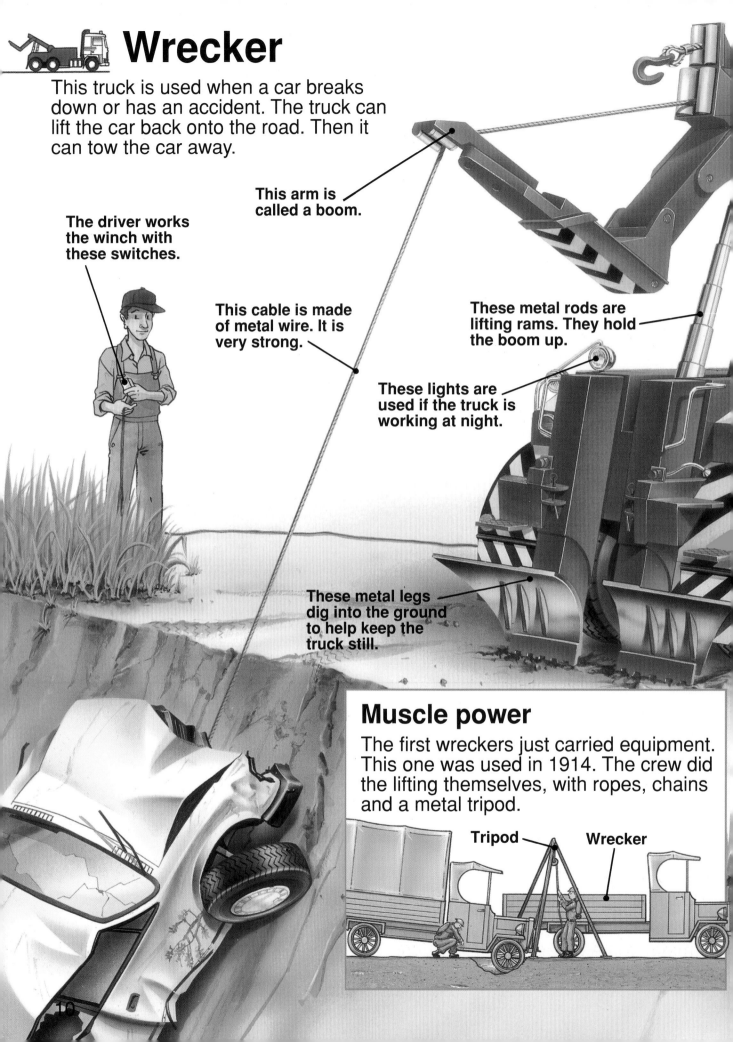

This drum is called a winch. It winds in the cable, pulling the car up.

Tools are kept in here.

This truck can lift loads as heavy as 12 big elephants.

Towing

The wrecker can tow things as big as itself, like this bus.

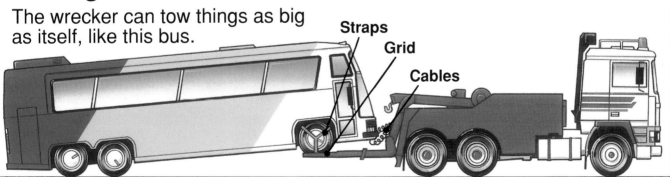

Straps

Grid

Cables

The bus's front wheels are lifted onto a metal frame called a grid. They are tied on with straps.

Cables carry power from the truck's engine to the bus. This makes the bus's brakes and lights work.

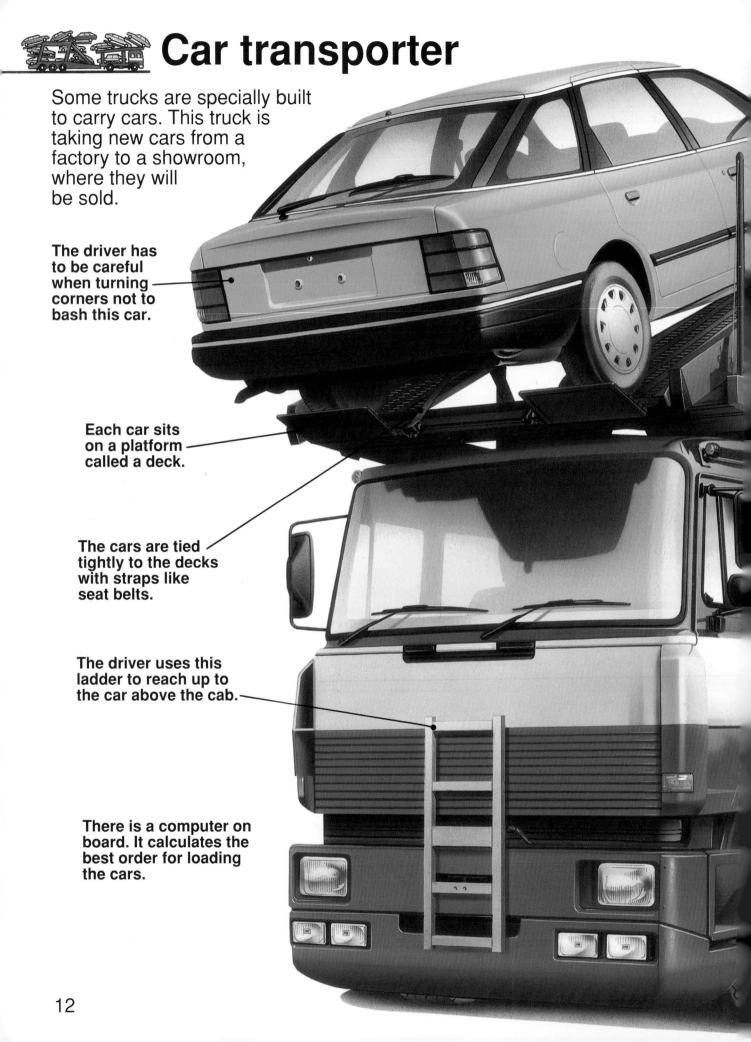

Car transporter

Some trucks are specially built to carry cars. This truck is taking new cars from a factory to a showroom, where they will be sold.

The driver has to be careful when turning corners not to bash this car.

Each car sits on a platform called a deck.

The cars are tied tightly to the decks with straps like seat belts.

The driver uses this ladder to reach up to the car above the cab.

There is a computer on board. It calculates the best order for loading the cars.

This transporter can carry 12 large cars.

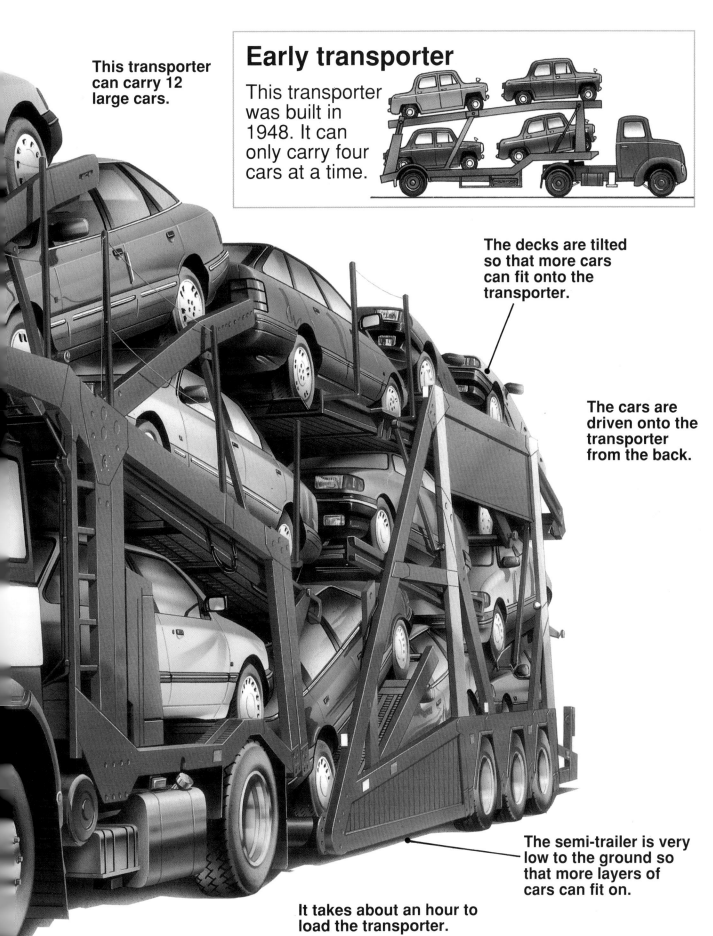

Early transporter

This transporter was built in 1948. It can only carry four cars at a time.

The decks are tilted so that more cars can fit onto the transporter.

The cars are driven onto the transporter from the back.

The semi-trailer is very low to the ground so that more layers of cars can fit on.

It takes about an hour to load the transporter.

Racing car transporter

This truck carries racing cars inside its big semi-trailer. When it gets to a race, the truck is used as a workshop. It carries all the tools and spare parts that might be needed to repair the cars.

Races are held all over the world, so the transporter travels vast distances every year.

The outside of the truck is painted with the name and colours of the racing team.

The cars have different types of tyres for dry and wet weather.

Spare wheels are kept inside these big lockers.

Inside the truck there is room for three cars. They are carried on two levels (see the opposite page).

The cars are lifted into and out of the truck on this platform.

The platform is moved using remote control switches.

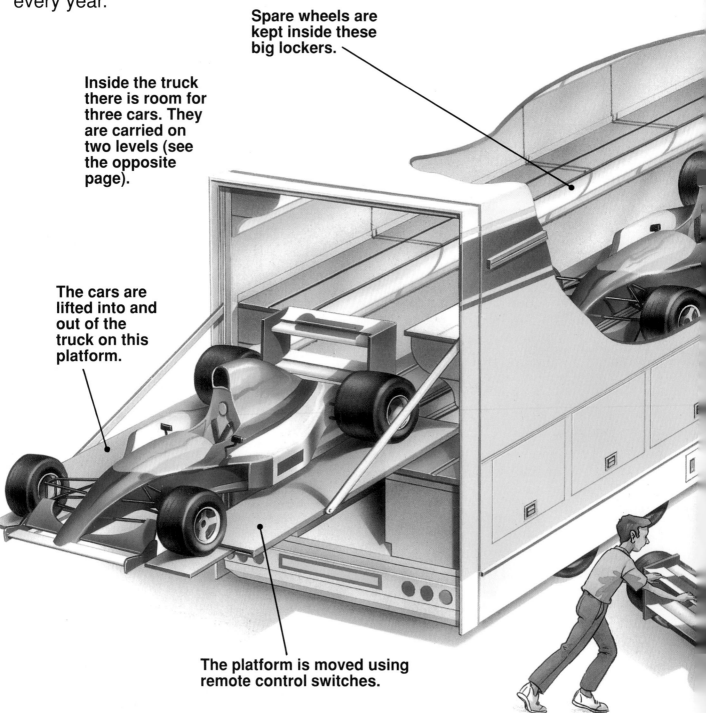

14

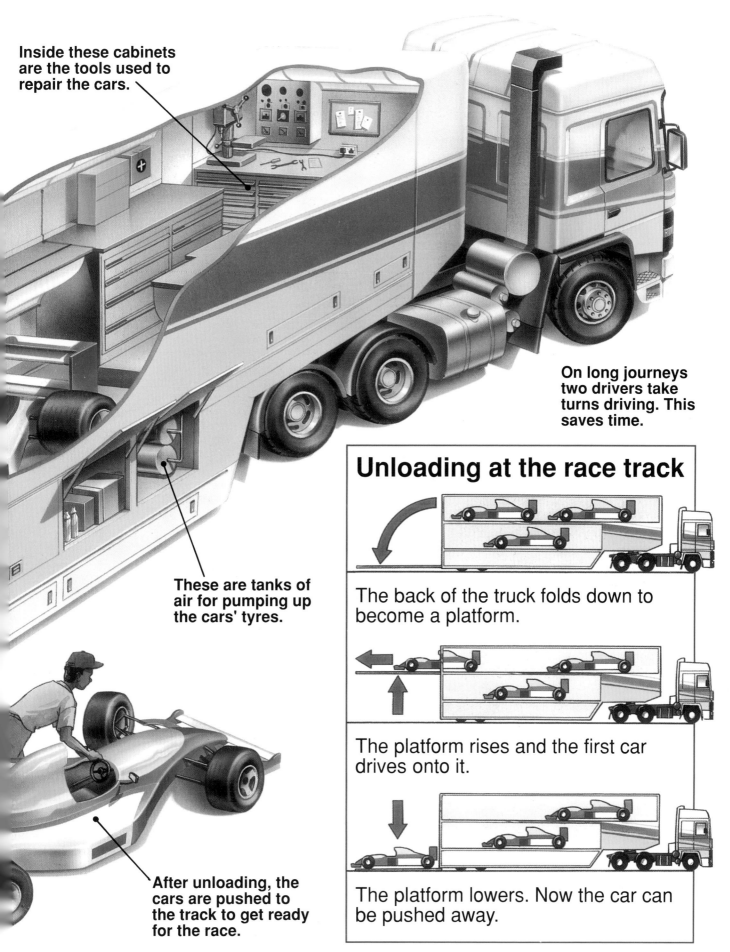

Inside these cabinets are the tools used to repair the cars.

On long journeys two drivers take turns driving. This saves time.

These are tanks of air for pumping up the cars' tyres.

After unloading, the cars are pushed to the track to get ready for the race.

Unloading at the race track

The back of the truck folds down to become a platform.

The platform rises and the first car drives onto it.

The platform lowers. Now the car can be pushed away.

15

Low-loader

A low-loader has a trailer which is low to the ground. This makes it easier to get the load on and off. It can carry very heavy things, such as this excavator.

These strips warn traffic that the truck is very long and wide.

Climbing on

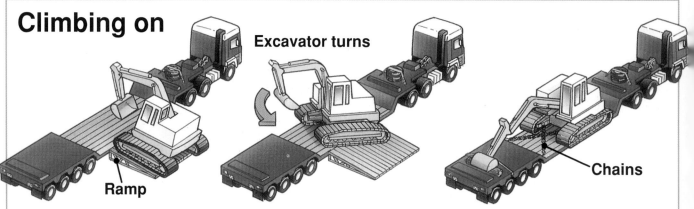

Excavator turns

Ramp

Chains

The excavator climbs up a ramp onto the trailer.

Then it turns on the spot to face the other way.

It is tied to the trailer with chains.

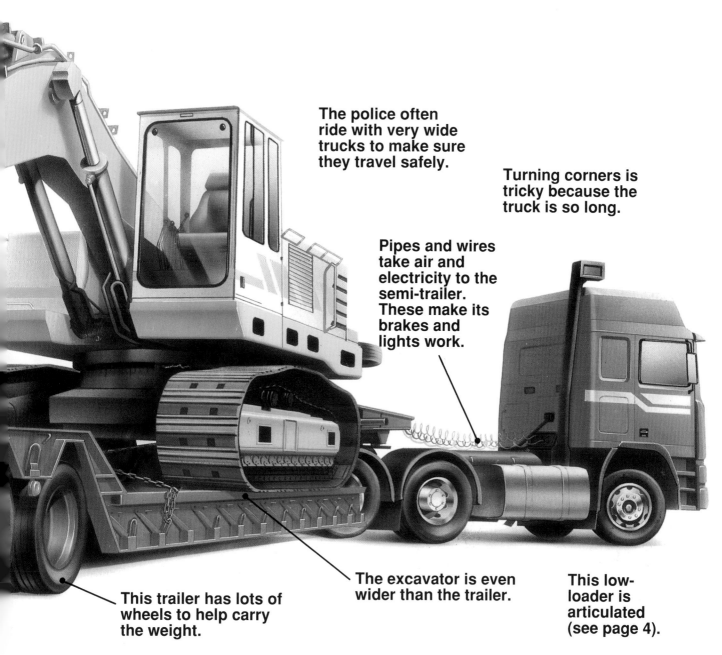

The police often ride with very wide trucks to make sure they travel safely.

Turning corners is tricky because the truck is so long.

Pipes and wires take air and electricity to the semi-trailer. These make its brakes and lights work.

The excavator is even wider than the trailer.

This trailer has lots of wheels to help carry the weight.

This low-loader is articulated (see page 4).

Space Shuttle truck

One of the largest loads carried by a truck is this Space Shuttle orbiter. The truck drives it to the launching pad.

The truck is specially designed to take the orbiter. It is only used for this job.

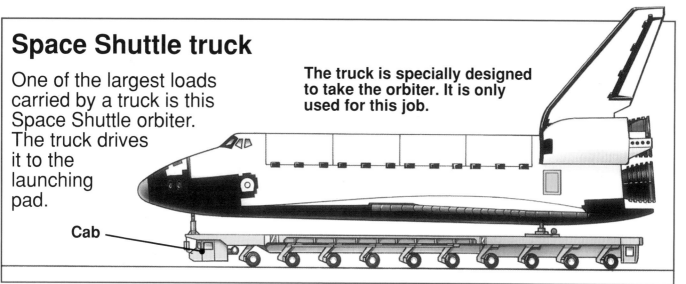

Cab

17

All-terrain truck

All-terrain trucks can drive over all sorts of ground without getting stuck. They have powerful engines and thick wheels. Their bodies are extra strong to stop them from getting damaged by rocky ground. This truck can load and unload itself, too.

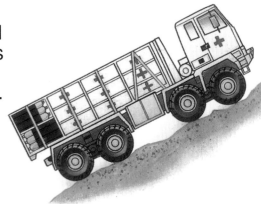

This truck can go up steep slopes, even with a heavy load.

Unloading

Rack

A metal arm lifts the rack and pushes it back until it touches the ground.

Arm

The truck drives out from underneath it.

Loading

The arm lifts the rack.

To load again, the arm lifts up the rack and the truck drives back under it.

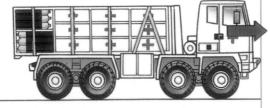

The truck drives away.

Then the arm pulls the rack up onto the truck's body and it is ready to drive away.

The load sits on a frame called a rack.

This truck is taking medical supplies across a desert. For most of the way there are no proper roads.

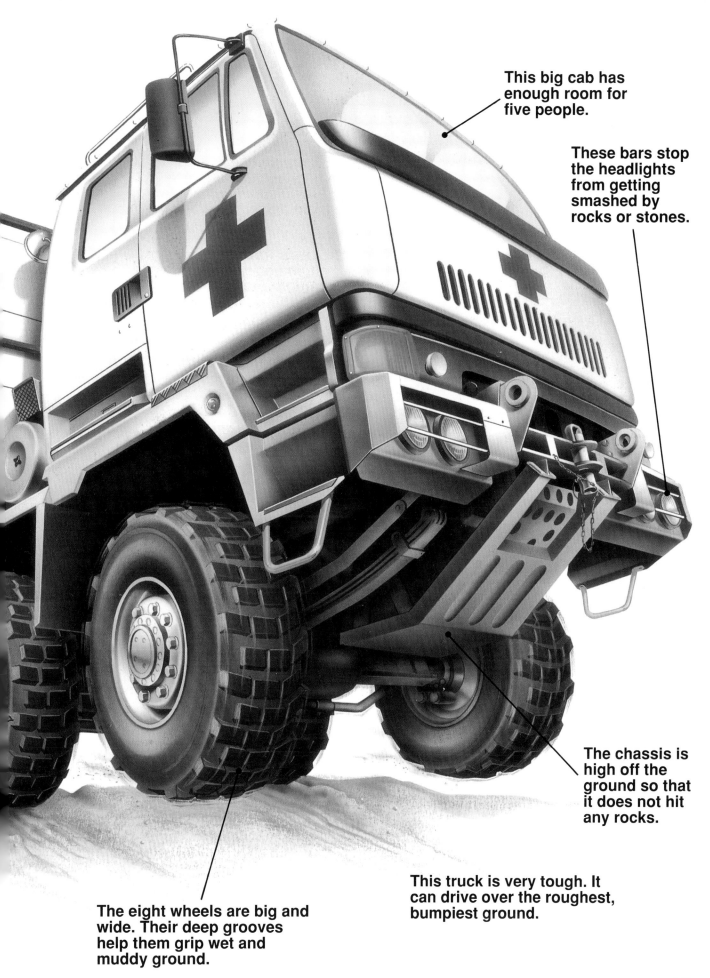

This big cab has
enough room for
five people.

These bars stop
the headlights
from getting
smashed by
rocks or stones.

The chassis is
high off the
ground so that
it does not hit
any rocks.

This truck is very tough. It
can drive over the roughest,
bumpiest ground.

The eight wheels are big and
wide. Their deep grooves
help them grip wet and
muddy ground.

Customized truck

This big truck has some of its outside parts covered in metals called chrome and stainless steel. These are very shiny, so they look good. Trucks with extra decoration like this are called customized trucks.

The driver has put extra lights on the cab for decoration.

Fumes from the engine come out here. It is called an exhaust stack.

Stainless steel

Cab shapes

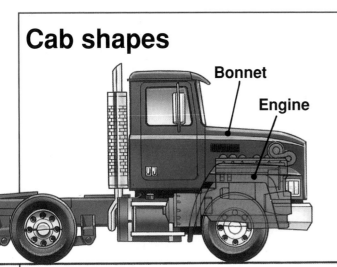

Bonnet

Engine

This truck has its engine in front of the cab, under a cover called a bonnet.

Engine

This truck has its cab on top of the engine. It is called a cab-over truck.

The tractor unit is very long. It rides smoothly over bumpy roads, so it is more comfortable for the driver.

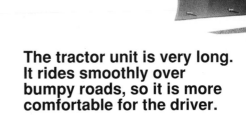

Big loads

These big trucks are powerful. They can pull all sorts of heavy loads in different types of semi-trailers. They often go on very long journeys.

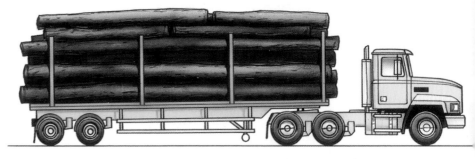

This truck is loaded with tree trunks.

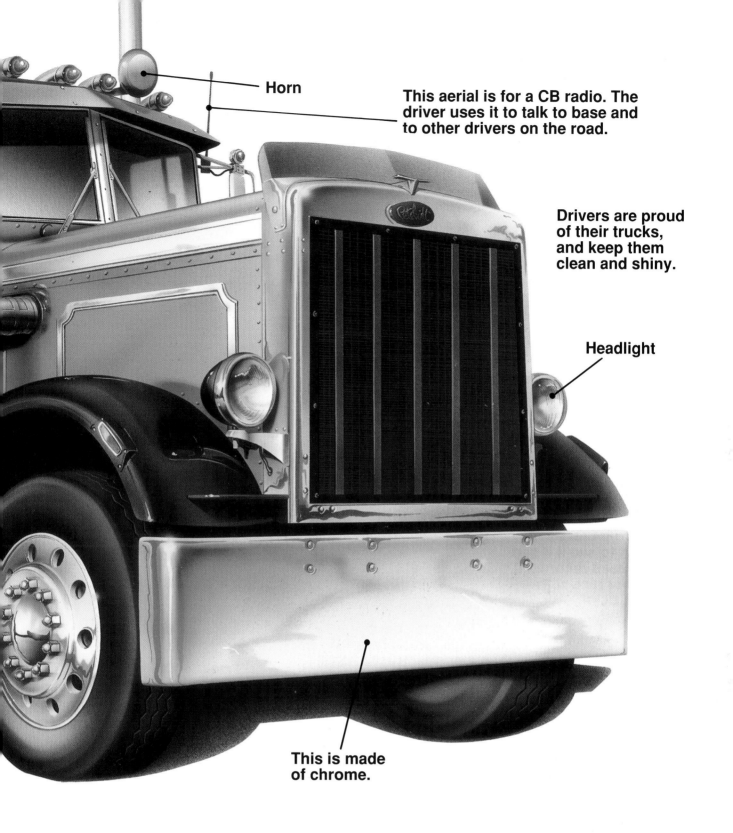

Horn

This aerial is for a CB radio. The driver uses it to talk to base and to other drivers on the road.

Drivers are proud of their trucks, and keep them clean and shiny.

Headlight

This is made of chrome.

This truck's semi-trailer is full of sand.   This truck is a giant tanker (see page 6).

Pro-jet truck

This is a racing truck. It is built for speed alone, so it is not used for carrying loads like normal trucks. It is called the Pro-jet truck because it has a jet engine taken from a fighter plane.

This truck has more pulling power than an express train.

These tubes have parachutes inside. They open out to help the truck slow down.

The Pro-jet races on its own to see if it can beat speed records. It does not race with other trucks.

The Pro-jet is about 100 times more powerful than a normal truck.

Truck racing

Sometimes the tractor units of normal trucks race against each other.

After going at top speed, it takes the truck about 500m (550yds) to be able to stop.

The drivers have to be very skilful to control the trucks when they are going fast.

The driver wears a helmet and a special suit. They protect him if there is an accident.

This truck's top speed is about 240km/h (150mph).

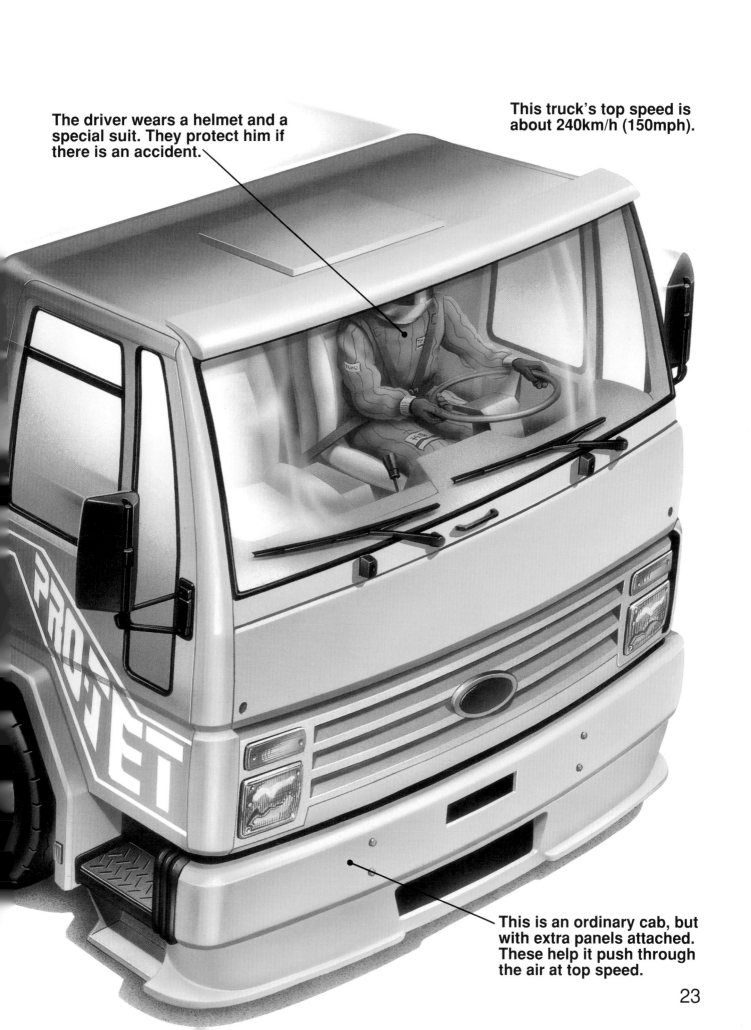

This is an ordinary cab, but with extra panels attached. These help it push through the air at top speed.

Fire truck

Trucks are very important in firefighting. They rush the firefighters to the fire. All the equipment they need is on board.

They have loud sirens for when they are in a hurry. These warn traffic on the roads to let them pass.

There is a tank inside the truck. It carries water for putting out the flames.

Ladders are kept on the roof. They are used for rescuing people.

This arm can stretch up very high. Its bright lights help the firefighters if it is dark or smoky.

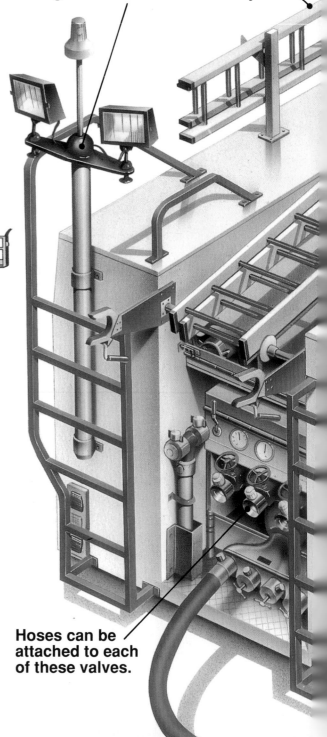

Hoses can be attached to each of these valves.

Special jobs

This all-terrain (see page 18) fire truck is used where driving is difficult, such as in forests and deserts.

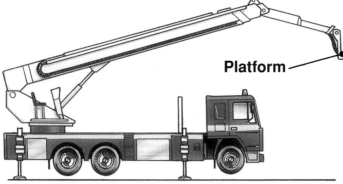

Platform

This fire truck raises and lowers a platform on its metal arm. It can reach up to the windows of tall buildings.

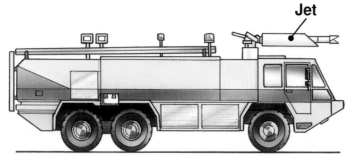

Jet

This fire truck stands by at the airport in case there is an accident. It has a strong water jet on the roof.

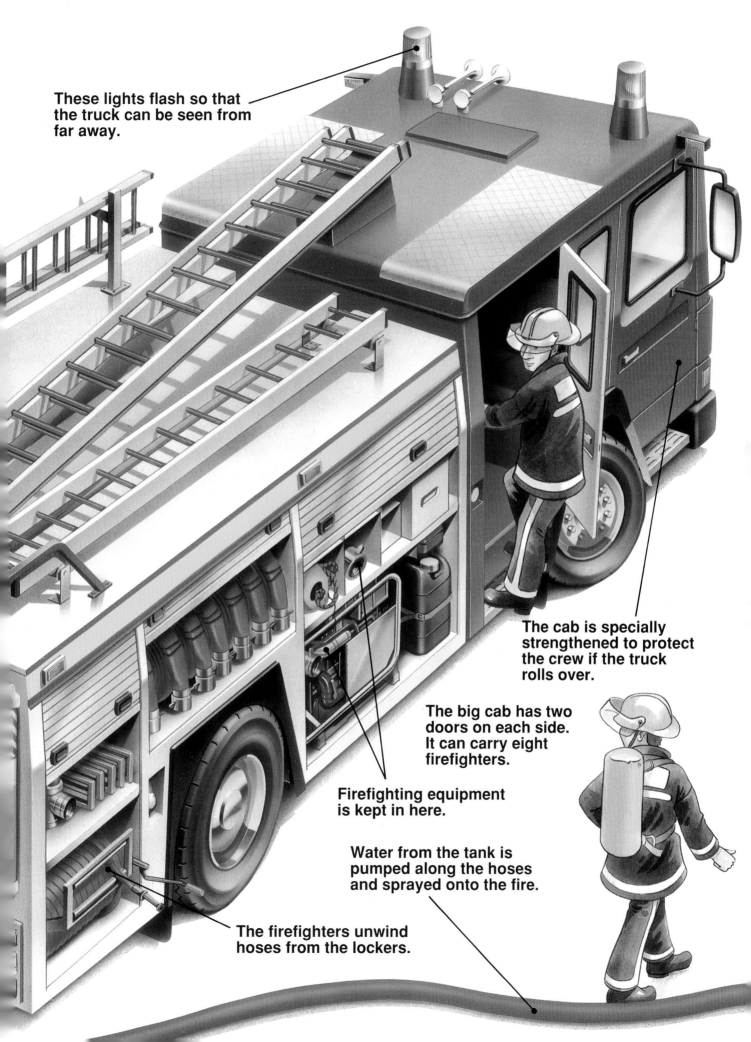

These lights flash so that the truck can be seen from far away.

The cab is specially strengthened to protect the crew if the truck rolls over.

The big cab has two doors on each side. It can carry eight firefighters.

Firefighting equipment is kept in here.

Water from the tank is pumped along the hoses and sprayed onto the fire.

The firefighters unwind hoses from the lockers.

Snowblower

In winter, this truck helps clear the roads so that other traffic can get through. It churns up the snow and blows it onto the side of the road.

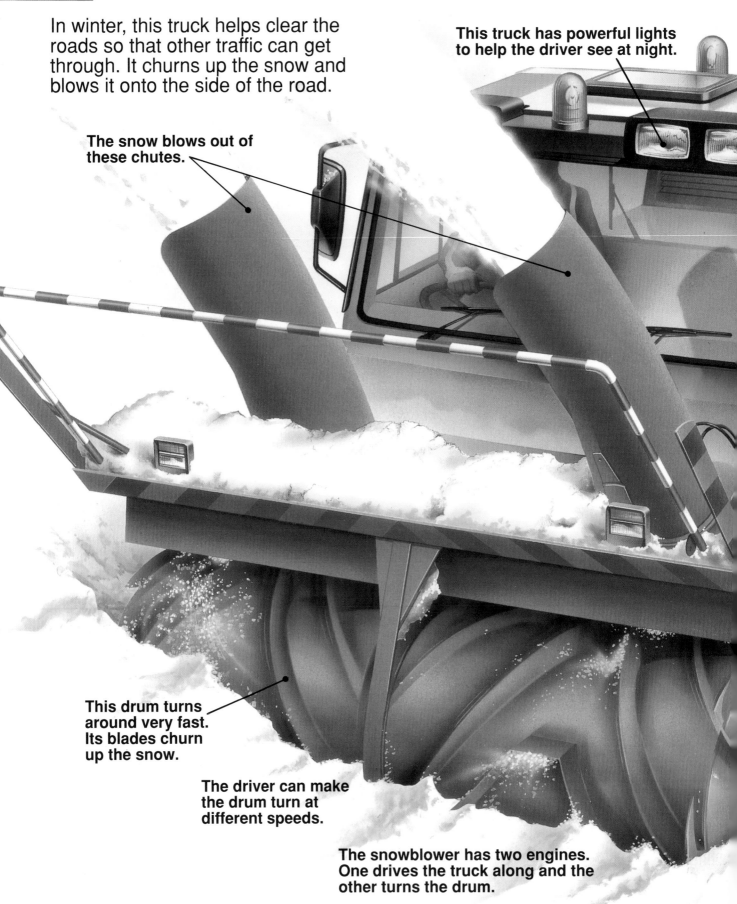

This truck has powerful lights to help the driver see at night.

The snow blows out of these chutes.

This drum turns around very fast. Its blades churn up the snow.

The driver can make the drum turn at different speeds.

The snowblower has two engines. One drives the truck along and the other turns the drum.

The cab is heated to keep the driver warm.

As the truck moves along, it clears a path through the snow.

These chains stop the wheels from slipping on the snow.

The cab has thick windows. These help block out noise from the engines and the blower.

How it works

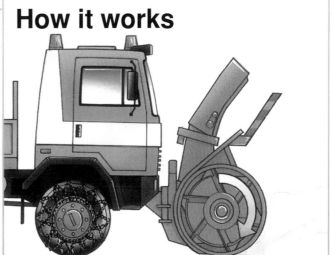

The drum's blades cut into the snow. As they spin, they fling the snow upward very hard.

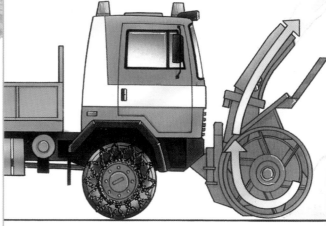

The snows flies out of the chutes. The truck moves forward, taking in more snow.

Snow plough

A snow plough clears snow by pushing it out of the way. It has a curved panel on the front called a face-plate.

Trucks from the past

Being a truck driver now is very different from seventy years ago. Trucks then were slower and less comfortable to ride in. They could not carry as much, either.

Steam truck

This truck was built in 1925. When it pulls its trailer, it can only travel at 8km/h (5mph), which is about the same speed as jogging.

This truck is driven by a steam engine. It gets its power by burning coal.

Bumpy ride

Early tyres were made of metal or wood. They were very bumpy to ride on.

Later, tyres were made of solid rubber.

Now tyres are filled with air, which cushions any bumps.

Delivery truck

This truck was built in the 1930s. The front of it looks very like the cars that were built at the same time.

The driver has to work this small wiper by hand.

The headlights stand out at the sides.

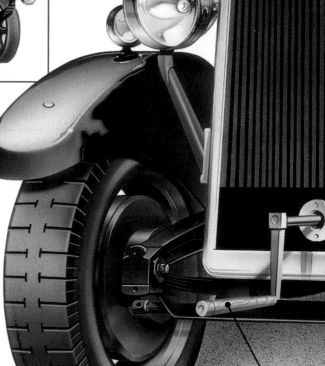

The driver has to turn this handle to start the engine.

This sheet is all that protects the load.

This truck is carrying bananas. Compare it with the truck on page 4.

The engine is in front of the cab, under a bonnet (see page 20).

The boxes have to be loaded and unloaded by hand.

 # Other trucks to spot

There are many different types of trucks to spot. How many can you find? What jobs are they doing? Here are some of the trucks you might see.

Skip truck

Trucks like this have containers on the back called skips or roll-offs. They collect waste from building sites.

Gully emptier

In many countries, you can see gully emptiers clearing the gullies, or drains, at the side of the road. They suck up the dirt through a long hose.

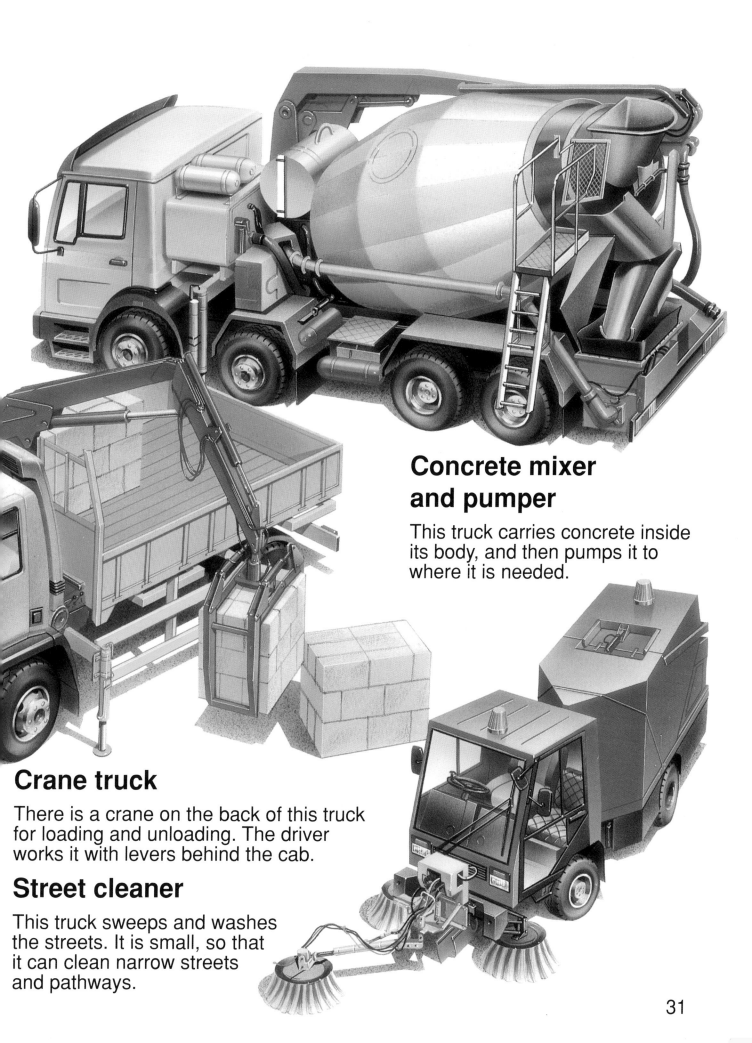

Concrete mixer and pumper

This truck carries concrete inside its body, and then pumps it to where it is needed.

Crane truck

There is a crane on the back of this truck for loading and unloading. The driver works it with levers behind the cab.

Street cleaner

This truck sweeps and washes the streets. It is small, so that it can clean narrow streets and pathways.

Index

With special thanks to: Commercial Motor magazine, Paul Chiltern, Peter Cramer, CSS Promotions Ltd, Adrian Graves, Robert Harris at Shell, Richard Hornsby, Steve Murty, NASA, John Philips, Pirelli, RARDE, Truck magazine, Williams Grand Prix Engineering Ltd.